MAGNETS

by Robin Nelson

first step nonfiction

ᒪ Lern... ...eapolis

Magnets make things move.

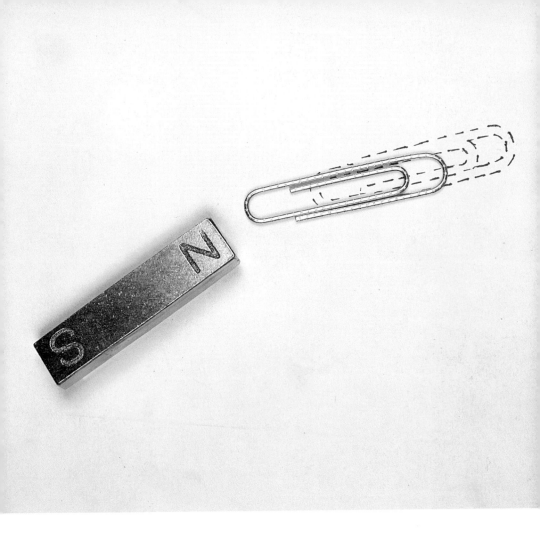

Magnets make things move
without touching them.

Most magnets are **metal.**

Magnets can make other
pieces of metal move.

Magnets pull things to them.

Magnets push things away
from them.

Magnets can move
paper clips.

Magnets can move pins.

Magnets cannot move
wood.

Magnets cannot move **plastic.**

Magnets help us build.

Magnets hold paper up.

Magnets help open cans.

Magnets keep toy trains
together.

Magnets help show us the way.

Magnets are everywhere.

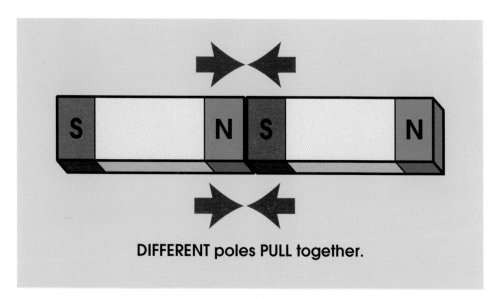

DIFFERENT poles PULL together.

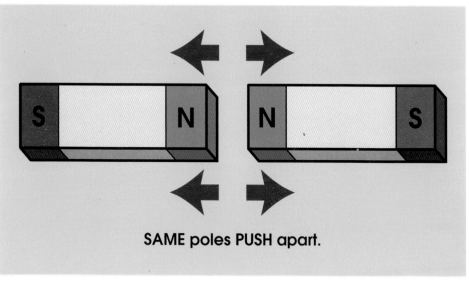

SAME poles PUSH apart.

18

Poles

Every magnet has two ends.
One end is called the north
pole. The other end is called
the south pole. The north pole
of one magnet will pull the
south pole of another magnet
toward it. The south pole of one
magnet will pull the north pole
of another magnet toward it.
The north pole of one magnet
will push the north pole of
another magnet away from it.
The south pole of one magnet
will push the south pole of
another magnet away from it.

Magnet Facts

 Magnets can only move things that are made out of certain metals, such as iron and steel.

 A magnet is strongest at its ends.

 A magnet can be made in any shape. Most magnets are shaped like bars or horseshoes.

Earth is a giant magnet.

 The needle in a compass is a magnet. The needle always points north.

 A rock called a lodestone is a natural magnet. Lodestones are made out of a mineral called magnetite.

Glossary

 magnets – metal that iron sticks to

 metal – something things are made of. Metal is usually shiny and hard. Metal comes from the ground.

 plastic – something things are made of. Plastic can be any color or shape. Plastic is made by people.

Index

The photographs in this book are reproduced through the courtesy of: © Todd Strand/Independent Picture Service, cover, pp. 2, 3, 4, 5, 6, 7, 8, 9, 10, 11, 12, 13, 14, 15, 22 (all); © Roger Ressmeyer/CORBIS, p. 16; Digital Vision Royalty Free, p. 17.

Illustration on p. 18 by Laura Westlund.

Lerner Publications Company
A division of Lerner Publishing Group
241 First Avenue North
Minneapolis, MN 55401 USA

Website address: www.lernerbooks.com

Library of Congress Cataloging-in-Publication Data

Nelson, Robin, 1971–
        Magnets / by Robin Nelson.
            p.   cm. — (First step nonfiction)
        Includes index.
        Summary: An introduction to magnets and how they work.
        ISBN: 0–8225–5132–2 (lib. bdg. : alk. paper)
        ISBN: 0–8225–5298–1 (pbk. : alk. paper)
        1. Magnets—Juvenile literature. 2. Magnetism—Juvenile literature. [1. Magnets.
    2. Magnetism.] I. Title. II. Series.
    QC753.7.N45   2004
    538'.4—dc22   2003013885

Manufactured in the United States of America
1 2 3 4 5 6 – DP – 09 08 07 06 05 04